# Dr. Dee Dee Dynamo's
# ICE WORM INTERVENTION

By

Il

Dr. Dee Dee Dynamo's Ice Worm Intervention
PRT0318A
Library of Congress Control Number: 2017919073
Printed in the United States
ISBN-13: 978-1-68401-841-3
www.mascotbooks.com

# DR. DEE DEE DYNAMO'S
# 5 HABITS OF POSITIVITY

1. There is *ALWAYS* a solution, *WORK* to find it!

2. *CONVERT* a limit into an *OPPORTUNITY*.

3. *KEEP* the *POSITIVE, DISCARD* the negative.

4. Find *PURPOSE* in *CARING* for others.

5. Be *THANKFUL* and *BELIEVE*!

## "Not Even The Sky Is The Limit!!"

"Holymackarolee!" exclaims Lukas, Dr. Dee Dee Dynamo's cousin and best friend. "I have never seen so much ice!"

Dr. Dee Dee Dynamo, Girl Super Surgeon, her family, and team peer through the airplane windows, marveling at the spectacular wintry icescape below.

"Cordova Ice Worm Festival, here we come!" Dr. Dee Dee says with anticipation.

"It seems unreal that there are worms that live in ice," says Lukas.

Dr. Dee Dee Dynamo was born on the Island of Positivity with super powers from electrical energy. She is a girl Super Hero who jets around the Universe fixing problems with her gifted hands. This is the Dynamo family's first vacation to Alaska, to visit a friend of Mommy Dynamo.

1

Kyle the Koala, Dr. Dee Dee's grumpy assistant, opens one eye and says sleepily, "Grrrrr, it's way too cold out there for me. I hope there will be no missions while we are here."

Dr. Dee Dee laughs, "I am always excited and prepared for a new mission, Kyle! No problem is too big or small, Dr. Dee Dee Dynamo can tackle them ALL!"

The Wilson Family is waiting eagerly in the Arrivals Lounge.

Amidst the hugs and laughter, Dr. Dee Dee notices a boy standing quietly.
"Hi, I'm Dee Dee," she says.

As the boy lowers his eyes, Mrs. Wilson looks over with affection.
"Dee Dee, this is our youngest son, Toby!"

Home of the
Cordova
Ice Worm Festival

FRESH DONUTS

Jacoby, Lukas' younger brother, runs over and enthusiastically envelops Toby in a bear hug.
"Nice to meet you, Toby!" he says. Toby hastily squirms out of Jacoby's embrace.

Jacoby is puzzled. Mrs. Wilson touches Toby gently and says, "Toby has autism which means that his brain processes differently. He doesn't speak much and does not express his feelings the same way you do. He is extremely smart but is not very talkative and doesn't like to be hugged."

"Bags are in the car," says Mr. Wilson. "Let's go home."

# It's Ice Worm Festival time!

Mommy Dynamo hustles the crew out of the house and reminds them, "Bundle up! It's much colder here than on the Island of Positivity!"

Mr. Wilson raves, "The highlight of your visit will be the Ice Worm Parade."

The kids arrive at the Festival and enthusiastically join the parade as the legs of the 140-foot-long Ice Worm which is weaving and winding its way down Main Street. Sounds of revelry are bursting forth from the Ice Worm and the crowd!

5

Suddenly, in the midst of the clamor, Dr. Dee Dee feels Wyndee Watch buzzing. Gordon the Gullible Globe, who can hear or sense whenever someone or something in the Universe is in distress, is spinning frantically on the screen.

ICE WORM FESTIVAL!

CORDOVA ICE WORM FESTIVAL

6

# WAHOO! WAHOO! WAHOO!

"What is it Gordon?" she asks.

"The Ice Worms are very upset," he responds.

Kyle, who has been snoozing on the side of the road, opens one eye and grumbles, "How do you know?"

"Maybe he heard them crying," suggests Marky Medicine Bag,
who carries Dr. Dee Dee's instruments.

Toby blurts out in a hushed tone. "Ice Worms don't make noises." The kids' eyes widen with surprise as they strain to hear him.

Mr. Wilson says to them, "Children with autism sometimes have learning disabilities but may be brilliant in one specific area. Toby knows everything about Ice Worms and climate change."

Toby continues quickly.

"Ice Worms:
~discovered in Alaska in 1887 on the Muir Glacier
~look like miniature earth worms
~live only in glacier ice
~ideal habitat temperature 32 degrees Fahrenheit
~melt and die at temperatures above 40 degrees Fahrenheit
~feed on snow algae and pollen grains trapped in the ice
~tunnel through the ice"

Dr. Dee Dee, Lukas, and Jacoby are speechless.

Gordon answers Kyle, "I can sense their extreme sadness. Their habitat is becoming too warm and they will die."

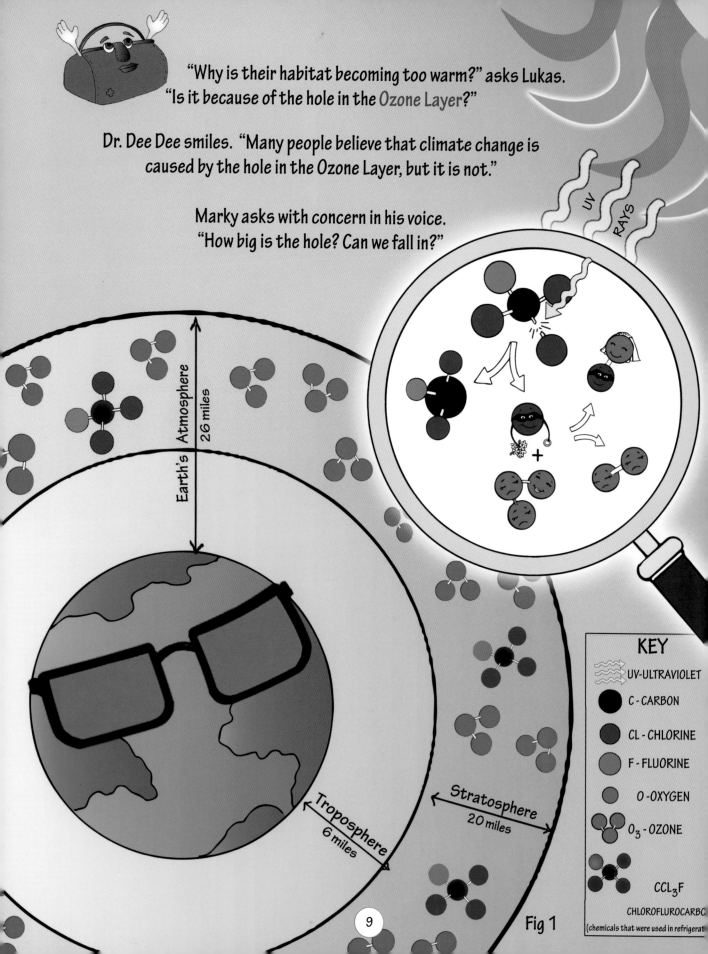

"Why is their habitat becoming too warm?" asks Lukas.
"Is it because of the hole in the Ozone Layer?"

Dr. Dee Dee smiles. "Many people believe that climate change is
caused by the hole in the Ozone Layer, but it is not."

Marky asks with concern in his voice.
"How big is the hole? Can we fall in?"

KEY

UV-ULTRAVIOLET

C - CARBON

CL - CHLORINE

F - FLUORINE

O - OXYGEN

$O_3$ - OZONE

$CCL_3F$

CHLOROFLUROCARBO

(chemicals that were used in refrigerat

Earth's Atmosphere 26 miles

Stratosphere 20 miles

Troposphere 6 miles

UV RAYS

9

Fig 1

# ~EARTH'S OZONE LAYER~

Earth's Atmosphere is the gas surrounding the Earth.

"No Marky," Dr. Dee Dee responds.
"It's not a real hole!"

Dr. Dee Dee explains,

The Ozone Layer is Earth's sunscreen,

protecting us from rays that cannot be seen.

Saving our eyes and our skin,

and also our immune system.

Then CFC came along,

Wanting so very much to belong.

Ultraviolet seized the opportunity,

And said, "I'll wipe out those Ozones that are blocking me!"

She conspired with the very sneaky Chlorine,

releasing him from the CFC scene.

Chlorine went off to steal from O3,

and eloped with one Oxygen in matrimony.

Leaving O2 confused and Earth difficult to console,

because the Ozone Layer now had a 'HOLE.'

"Well, enough of that," said the authorities,

and restricted CFC like a dog with fleas.

Ultraviolet, you will not have your way,

Earth is relieved, the 'HOLE' is shrinking,

## Hip Hip HOORAY!!!

Use figure 1 to Answer Questions

1. Name the 2 parts of Earth's atmosphere

2. How wide is the Earth's atmosphere?

| KEY | ANSWER |
|---|---|
| CFC - Chlorofluorocarbon | |
| O2 - Oxygen | 2, 26 miles |
| O3 - Ozone | 1. Troposphere, Stratosphere |

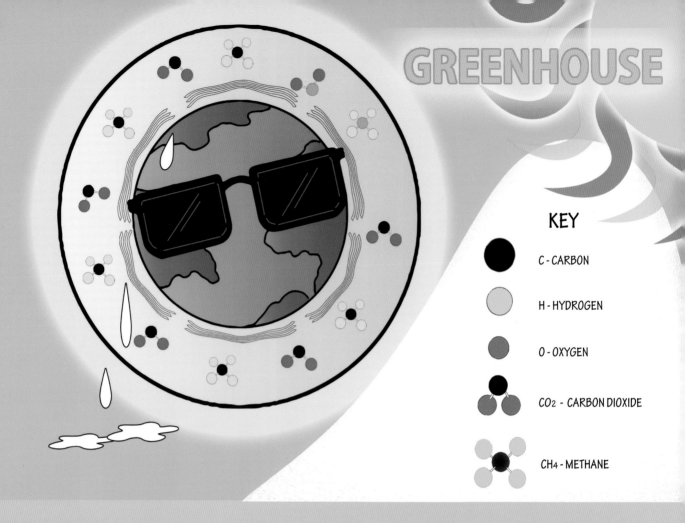

**KEY**

C - CARBON

H - HYDROGEN

O - OXYGEN

CO₂ - CARBON DIOXIDE

CH₄ - METHANE

"Does anyone know why the Ice Worm habitat is warming up?" asks Marky.

After a long pause Toby speaks. "The Earth's atmosphere has 5 layers, but the one closest to Earth, the troposphere, behaves like a giant greenhouse. When the Sun's rays reach Earth, Earth warms up. At night, as Earth cools down, heat is released and trapped. This causes the temperature of Earth to rise. This is called the Greenhouse Effect and is causing the glaciers where Ice Worms live to warm up and melt. The gases that trap the heat are called greenhouse gases. Carbon dioxide is the most common."

"Are greenhouse gases all bad?" asks Lukas.

Dr. Dee Dee responds, "No Lukas. Greenhouse gases protect our planet from freezing, but too many will cause the planet to become very hot, like Venus."

EFFECT

Greenhouse gases are:

- carbon dioxide
- methane
- nitrous oxide
- water vapor

Reasons for increased greenhouse gases

-increase in the burning of fossil fuels
(oil, coal, natural gas) for
electricity, energy for heat,
and transportation
-loss of forests because of
construction, farming, and
other development

Z-Z-Z-Z-Z-Z-Z

## EFFECTS OF CLIMATE CHANGE

Marky asks, "If we know what's causing the problem, why don't we fix it, like we did for the hole in the Ozone Layer?"

Dr. Dee Dee replies, "Some people don't want to believe that human activity is the cause of the increase in Earth's temperature."

"What will happen if we don't change?" Jacoby asks Dr. Dee Dee.

Toby whispers, "Weather will change, climate will become hotter in some places and colder in others. Glaciers will melt and the sea level will rise. Some places will have disastrous floods and some places will experience devastating droughts. Some plants, animals, and even people will not survive. Our earth may become uninhabitable."

Kyle mumbles incredulously, "This guy is a walking encyclopedia."

**MELTING GLACIERS**

**DROUGHTS**

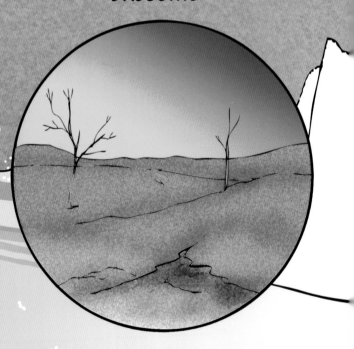

FLOODS

DYING CORAL REEFS

EXTINCTION OF
SOME ANIMALS

14

Lukas asks, "Can you fix this Dr. Dee Dee?"

"There is **ALWAYS** a solution! We will **WORK** to find it," responds Dr. Dee Dee.

She speaks into Wyndee Watch and sends a signal to Freeda the Flying Ambulance. Freeda can whisk Dr. Dee Dee and the team anywhere in the Universe. "Mobilize the team and bring Scotty Suction and the Technology Twins."

"Why does Scotty Suction have to come?" grumbles Kyle. "I dislike that loud noise he makes whenever he suctions, and he's always sucking up my leaves."

"He is an important part of the surgical team," responds Dr. Dee Dee. "You two will figure out how to work together!"

Habit of Positivity #1
THERE IS ALWAYS
A SOLUTION.

She says to the Technology Twins, "Can you design an Air Purification System that removes excess carbon dioxide from the atmosphere?"

"Absolutely!" the Technology Twins respond.

"Holymackarolee! We are going to build a huge air vacuum cleaner!" grins Lukas.

Dr. Dee Dee claps her hands with glee. "You are exactly right, Lukas! Enter Scotty Suction!"

"This sounds way too simple," mutters Kyle. "If it were that easy, wouldn't someone have done this already?"

Dr. Dee Dee answers, "The simple solution would be for humans to use more clean energy, plant more trees, and stop using fossil fuels. The Air Purification System is more complex and will need my Super Hero powers."

Habit of Positivity #4
BE THANKFUL AND
BELIEVE

Freeda sets the GPS and takes off.

Gordon says with a panicked tone, "The Ice Worms don't think they can wait, and Freeda always gets lost."

Dr. Dee Dee smiles. "Freeda BELIEVES that she will arrive at her destination and she always does, in spite of the detours!"

Kyle says to Gordon, "The Ice Worms will need to be patient."

"Oh Kyle! We must get to them as soon as possible," declares Dr. Dee Dee.

She speaks into Wyndee Watch. "Where are you, Freeda?"

Freeda responds sheepishly. "The GPS set course for 'Glaciers
with Ice Worms' and directed us to the Northern Cascade Glacier in British Columbia."

Kyle groans. "What in the world are you doing in British Columbia?"

Toby says quietly, "There are only four glaciers where Ice Worms live.
They are located in Alaska, British Columbia, Oregon, and Washington."

Map of Ice Worm Locations

Ice Worms live in...

A. Chugach Mountain
B. Glacier Bay Region
C. Coastal Range
D. Cascades Mountain Range
E. Olympic Mountains

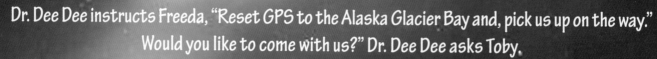

Dr. Dee Dee instructs Freeda, "Reset GPS to the Alaska Glacier Bay and, pick us up on the way."
Would you like to come with us?" Dr. Dee Dee asks Toby.

He adamantly shakes his head no.

Jacoby says, "I will stay here with Toby."

Lukas asks Toby, "Will we be able to see an Ice Worm?"

Mrs. Wilson says to Lukas, "Toby won't speak if you address him directly."

Lukas rephrases, "I wonder if we will be able to see an Ice Worm."

Toby says, "Ice Worms are very small, maybe the size of a long eyelash. It is unlikely that you will see a single Ice Worm. There are billions of them living in the glacier. When the sun goes down, they will crawl towards the surface to eat, and appear as a shadow in the glacier ice."

Dr. Dee Dee, Kyle, Lukas, and Marky join the Technology Twins
on board Freeda and jet off to the glaciers.

I'm Dr. Dee Dee Dynamo,
Super Surgeon ON THE GO!
My hands were made to heal.
I cut, I sew, I tie with zeal;
No problem is too big or small,
Dr. Dee Dee Dynamo can tackle them all!

ICE WORM

Dr. Dee Dee uses her SUPER
POWERS and decreases the
temperature in the glaciers.

**WAHOO! WAHOO! WAHOO!**

Gordon is spinning frantically.

"What is it Gordon?" Dr. Dee Dee asks.

"Roars are coming from Arctic animals who also want an immediate solution," he responds.

Polar bears, narwhals, and walruses are stampeding across the ice towards Freeda. Dr. Dee Dee quickly erects an electromagnetic field to protect Freeda and the team from being trampled. She raises her hands to calm the animals.

"What do you need?" she asks gently. A gigantic walrus lumbers forward and says, "Our sea ice is melting. The ice provides us with food and protection. When we are forced to live on land we are unable to get our food from the water and our predators can hunt us more easily."

Kyle says irritably, "We can only do one Mission at a time."

"Not even the Sky is the Limit, Kyle!" Dr. Dee Dee says brightly. "I am POSITIVE that we can find a way to help the Arctic animals too."

She checks the charge on Wyndee Watch and has just enough power to help the Arctic animals. She launches into the air and directs her powerful hands to refreeze large areas of ocean ice.

The Technology Twins complete the design of the Air Purification System. Dr. Dee Dee places the material for the filtration panels on Freeda's surgical table. Her fingers are literally tingling!

"Let's go," she says to the instruments and she begins the task of sewing the filtration panels which are **infused** with a **reagent** that will bind the carbon in the carbon dioxide molecule.

She sews together a huge dome and installs the filtration panels. She positions Scotty Suction at the top and connects him. The Technology Twins have built a motor which releases the clean air back into the atmosphere.

"How will we know if this works?" asks Marky.

"We can test the air as it exits but we will have to be patient," responds Dr. Dee Dee. "We also need to do our part by conserving, using clean energy and replanting trees wherever we cut them down."

"Do we have to leave Scotty Suction behind?" Marky asks sadly.

"He is fulfilling his destiny," Dr. Dee Dee reassures him. "We will return for him when his work is done."

The team flies back to Cordova where Toby is waiting.
His shoulders visibly relax as the team lands, even though he remains silent.

Dr. Dee Dee says to Toby:

Marky Medicine Bag, who has been scribbling furiously while
Dr. Dee Dee has been speaking, steps out of Freeda.
"I have made a replica of me and written all the POSITIVE
things Dr. Dee Dee said to you. I'm placing them in your bag
so you can always remember how valuable you are."

"You are brilliant.
We have learned so much
from you
and could not have
done this without you.
You have helped us
save our planet."

DELIVERIES

CORDOVA ALASKA
AIRPORT

WELCOME

CORDOVA
GIFT SHOP

DR. DEE DEE
DYNAMO

SCOTTIE SUCTION

TECHNOLOGY
TWINS

MARKY MEDICINE BAG

TOBY

JACOBY

KYLE

LUKAS

Dr. Dee Dee applauds. "Perfect! Affirmations are the tools that help you to develop the HABITS of POSITIVITY! You now have your own Marky Medicine Affirmation Bag!"

"Thank you, Dr. Dee Dee," says Mrs. Wilson. "We will keep filling the bag, and someday Toby will fill it on his own."

Gordon flashes on the screen. "The Ice Worms are emitting feelings of gratitude and joy and the Arctic animals are extremely grateful."

Mommy Dynamo says, "Another job well done, Dr. Dee Dee Dynamo—Super Surgeon on the Go!!! Planet Earth thanks you!"

FREEDA

THE CHARGER FAMILY

MOMMY AND DADDY DYNAMO

GRANDMA B

GRANDDAD WILLY

MR. AND MRS. WILSON

THE END

# GLOSSARY WORDS

**Atmosphere** – gases surrounding Earth or another planet. Earth's atmosphere is divided into 5 layers, starting closest to Earth—troposphere, stratosphere, mesosphere, thermosphere, exosphere—and gases become thinner with each layer.

**Autism** – Autism Spectrum Disorder (ASD) is a developmental disorder that causes difficulties with social interaction, communication, language, and motor skills. Individuals may also exhibit repetitive behaviors. It is a life-long condition and symptoms vary widely.

**Carbon Dioxide** – a colorless gas that is produced when humans and animals breathe out, or when certain fuels are burned. It is used by plants for photosynthesis.

**Chlorine** – a very reactive element that is a greenish yellow irritating gas which has a strong odor and is used as bleach, as a disinfectant to purify water, and to make other products such as textiles and plastics.

**Chlorofluorocarbon** – a compound that contains carbon, chlorine, fluorine, and sometimes hydrogen. It is used in refrigeration, as a solvent, and in aerosol sprays. It is believed to cause ozone loss in the stratosphere.

**Clean Energy** – also known as renewable energy, which does not pollute the earth's atmosphere when used, e.g., solar, wind, waves.

**Climate Change** – refers to the increase in Earth's average surface temperature resulting in changing climate on the planet.

**Cordova** – a small city in the state of Alaska which has been home to the Ice Worm Festival since 1961.

**Encyclopedia** – a reference resource (such as a book, series of books) that contains detailed information on topics arranged alphabetically.

**Fahrenheit** – a temperature scale developed by Daniel Gabriel Fahrenheit which bases the boiling point of water at 212 °F and the freezing point at 32 °F.

**Filtration** – the process of passing a liquid or gas through a filter to remove solid particles.

**Greenhouse Effect** – relating to or caused by the warming of the Earth's atmosphere because of the trapping of heat by gases in Earth's atmosphere.

**Habitat** – the place where a plant or animal grows or lives in nature, or a place where people live.

**Ice Worm** – earthworm-like, fine, black creatures, a few centimeters long that live on ice glaciers. They are one of the 77 species in the Mesenchytraeus genus and the only one to live in glacier ice. They survive on algae, pollen grains, and their body functions—reproduction, metabolism, growth—all occur at the freezing mark, at about 32° Fahrenheit (0° Celsius).

**Immune System** – the system in human bodies that protects us from infection and disease. It is made up of specialized organs (e.g., thymus and spleen), cells (e.g., white blood cells), and tissues (e.g., lymph nodes) that all work together to destroy these invaders.

Methane – an odorless gaseous compound that is the main constituent of natural gas and is also produced by decomposition of organic matter in places like landfills and swamps. In 2015, it accounted for 10% of all U.S. greenhouse gas emissions from human activity. It contains 4 Hydrogens and 1 Carbon ($CH_4$).

Nitrous Oxide – commonly known as laughing gas, it is a colorless, odorless gas that is used by dentists especially for sedation. It occurs naturally in the atmosphere and is also produced by human activities such as agriculture, fossil fuel combustion, and industrial processing. It is a greenhouse gas that has a warming potential that is 310 times carbon dioxide. It contains 2 Nitrogens and 1 Oxygen ($N_2O$).

Oxygen - a colorless, odorless gas that makes up 20% of Earth's atmosphere and is essential for life.

Ozone Layer - the ozone layer prevents most ultraviolet (UV) and other high-energy radiation from penetrating to the Earth's surface but does allow through sufficient ultraviolet rays to support the activation of vitamin D in humans.

Purification – the removal of contaminants.

Reagent – a substance used in a chemical reaction to detect, measure, examine, or produce other substances.

Stratosphere – an upper portion of the atmosphere extending from about 6 miles (10 kilometers) to 30 miles (50 kilometers) upward where temperature changes little and clouds rarely form.

Troposphere – the lowest layer of atmosphere, within which there is a steady drop in temperature with increasing altitude and within nearly all cloud formations occur and weather conditions manifest themselves.

Ultraviolet Rays – radiation produced by the Sun; wave lengths shorter than visible light but longer than x-rays. It is extremely dangerous to living things.

Venus – the hottest planet that is second in order from the Sun. It has a very thick atmosphere that is 100 times more massive than Earth's and is made up primarily of carbon dioxide causing a very significant greenhouse effect.

Water Vapor – the gaseous state of water in the atmosphere produced by the evaporation or boiling of liquid water and can appear as mist or steam.

# LEARNING WORDS

Adamant – sticking to an opinion or refusing to be persuaded or change one's mind

Affirmation – encouraging words; confirming something to be true

Assembles – to put together separate parts of an object; to gather together

Avert – to turn away; to prevent

Clamor – very loud noise made by a lot of people or things

Conserve –to protect; to prevent waste

Console - comfort

Conspire – make secret plans

Declines – politely refuse (an invitation or offer) or become smaller or decrease

Devastating – highly destructive or damaging

Elope – secretly run away to get married

Emit – to flow out, issue, proceed, or come forth

Envelops – wrap up, cover, or surround completely

Gigantic – of very great size; huge or enormous

Glee – great delight

Hastily – quickly

Icescape – an area covered with ice or with snow and ice

Incredulously – showing disbelief

Infused –to soak something in a liquid to extract the flavors from it

Launch – a sudden energetic movement; send into orbit; throw forcefully

Licorice – a dark colored candy flavored by the dried root of the Licorice plant

Lumbers – move in a heavy, slow way

Marveling – filled with amazement or wonder

Matrimony – marriage

Mobilize – to bring (people) together for action

Peer – to look closely

Predators – an animal that naturally hunts, kills, and eats other animals

Raves – speak about something with great enthusiasm; talk wildly

Replica - copy

Restrict– put a limit on

Revelry – lively and noisy festivities; a wild, fun time

Sheepishly – embarrassed or bashful, by having done something wrong or foolish

Sidles – to go or move with one side forward

Squirms – wiggle or twist the body from side to side

Stampede – sudden panicked rush of animals or people

Trampled – tread heavily with the feet so as to crush, bruise, or destroy

Uninhabitable – not suitable for living in

RESOURCE GUIDE

Autism

**Autism Speaks – www.autismspeaks.org**
**U.S. National Library of Medicine – www.medlineplus.gov**

Climate Change

**NASA Global Climate Change – www.climate.nasa.gov**

**National Geographic – www.nationalgeographic.com**

Greenhouse Gases

**Environmental Protection Agency – www.epa.gov**

Ozone Layer

**Environmental Protection Agency – www.epa.gov**

Ice Worm image used with permission of the
Cordova Festival Committee.

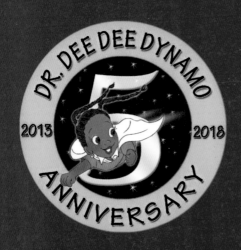

info@drdeedeedynamo.com
www.drdeedeedynamo.com